Be A Good Dragon

By Kurt Cyrus

PUBLISHED BY SLEEPING BEAR PRESS

Sleeping Bear Press™

2395 South Huron Parkway, Suite 200, Ann Arbor, MI 48104
www.sleepingbearpress.com
© Sleeping Bear Press

Printed and bound in China
10 9 8 7 6 5 4 3 2 1
Library of Congress Cataloging-in-Publication Data
Names: Cyrus, Kurt, author, illustrator.
Title: Be a good dragon / written and illustrated by Kurt Cyrus.
Description: Ann Arbor, MI : Sleeping Bear Press, [2018] | Summary:
"When a dragon catches a cold, setting off fires with its sneezes, a wizard
comes to the rescue with a magic potion"—Provided by the publisher.
Identifiers: LCCN 2017029796 | ISBN 9781585363834
Subjects: | CYAC: Stories in rhyme. | Dragons—Fiction. | Sick—Fiction. |
Sneezing—Fiction. | Cold (Disease)—Fiction. | Wizards—Fiction. | Magic—Fiction.
Classification: LCC PZ8.3.C997 Be 2018 | DDC [E]—dc23
LC record available at https://lccn.loc.gov/2017029796

When cinders come showering
down from the skies . . .

And thunder is rumbling,

and smoke burns your eyes . . .

Then run like a rabbit! Fly like the breeze!

Enzo the dragon is starting to sneeze.

"Ka-Chee! Ka-Choo!
        ker-Splabble-dee-Sploo!"

The mountain is splattered with crackling goo.

**"I'b sick! I'b sick!
Oh, Baba, be quick!"**
He sprays an explosion of sparkling ick.

His mother says,
"Please, cover your sneeze.
No one is eager to catch your disease."

But Enzo explodes in a terrible roar:

"Id's drivigg be duts! I CAD DAKE EDDY BORE!"

Warn all the people! Sound the alarm!
Pack up your piggies and flee from your farm!
Enzo is coming. He's headed this way,
fouling the air with his sulfurous spray.

Creating a storm with his sneezes and sniffs,
Enzo comes hurtling over the cliffs.
Over the boulders, over the snow,
straight for the fields and the pastures below!

The farmers are running. They're fleeing their shacks
with cows in their carts and kids on their backs.

Their crops are all wilting—
Their corn is all popping—

"Ker-SPLIFF!" Enzo says.

And he *still* isn't stopping!

"Enzo is coming!" the villagers shriek.
"Run for the river! Jump in the creek!"

EEEK!

The royal magician appears on the scene:
"I come in the name of the king and the queen!"
(He's barely awake as he stumbles outside.
His robe is on backward. His shoes are untied.)

"Bake be all bedder!" the dragon demands.
The wizard starts chanting and waving his hands.

"Abracadabra! The thing I suggest
is plenty of fluids and plenty of rest!"

Enzo goes **BLAT**
and scorches his hat.

"Sorry!" says Enzo. "Eggscuse be for dat."

Jesters and jokers arrive in a wagon
with buckets of water to throw at the dragon.
The water, midstream, is turned into steam.
"Our weapons are useless!" the jokers all scream.

"Here," says the wizard. "I brought you a drink.
It's just about time for your nap, I should think."

"I DODE DEED A DAP!" the dragon complains,
lighting up avenues, alleys, and lanes.

The knights on the street
refuse to retreat.
They gallop ahead without missing a beat. . . .

"Ka-CHOO! Ka-CHOO!"

There's no getting through.
They cover their faces—what else can they do?

"Wait!" says the wizard. "All righty. You win.
Kalamazoo. Let the magic begin!"
He whips up a tubful of abraca-brew
and conjures a magical pillow or two.

"**Thag you**," says Enzo. He drains the whole batch—
two hundred gallons—
     right down the hatch.

Plenty of fluids—that's a good start!
     Plenty of rest is the second part.
"Sleep," says the wizard. "When I count to four . . ."

     Enzo replies with a rumbling snore.

And when he awakens, the sneezes are beat.
He lets out a burp as he gets to his feet,
then slishes and sloshes away to the hills,
foggy and groggy and full to the gills.

If *you* catch a sniffle, then here's what to do:

Drink a few gallons of abraca-brew
and lie on a magical bed for a spell.
Abracadabra! It works pretty well.

And if you should feel that you're starting to sneeze,
be a good dragon.
Cover it, please.